HIDE AND SEEK

Hide and Seek

by DOROTHY CLEWES

Illustrated by Sofia

COWARD-McCANN, INC.
NEW YORK

CONTENTS

HIDE AND SEEK

THE INVITATION

PENNY'S mother put down the letter she was reading and looked across the table at Penny.

"Maxwell's mother wants you to spend a day on the farm with them," she said.

Penny stopped in the middle of taking the top off the large brown egg she was having for breakfast.

"When?" she said.

Her mother looked at the letter again. "Tomorrow," she said. "Maxwell's father will come for you on his way back from the market."

Maxwell was eight, which was a little older

than Penny. He was the first friend she had made when her mother and father had come to live in the new town — that is, he was her first friend if you didn't count the postman and the milkman. Once when they had been walking over the fields together he had pointed the farm out to her. It had looked just like all the farms in her picture books and she wanted very much to go and play there.

Now the invitation had come and she didn't know how she could wait until tomorrow morning. It was like waiting for a birthday — except that instead of new toys to play with there would be real live animals: Maxwe'lls dog, Prince; the cats, the ducks, the geese, the cows, the pigs and the horses.

All day long she could think of nothing else. After dinner, when her mother said, "Time for bed, Penny," she didn't try to think of an excuse. She was upstairs and between the sheets before you could say Penelope, which was Penny's real name.

Under the sheets she closed her eyes tightly and at once she could see the farm as she had seen it

from the hillside above the fields that day with Maxwell. It was snuggled under the hills as warmly as she was snuggled under the blankets — a long, low, sprawling house with smoke curling up from its chimneys. It had sheds and barns and stables around it. In the fields close by there were haystacks and gaily colored carts and wagons. She had sat with Maxwell on the hillside looking down on the farm and he had told her all about the animals living there: the cows in the sheds, the horses in the stables, and the hens scratching about in the grain-filled barns and laying large eggs in the soft straw. Tomorrow she would see it all, for herself. Tomorrow she would play with them all. Now she would go to sleep and when she woke up it would be The Day.

Sunshine pouring through her bedroom window woke Penny early. Now she only had to get dressed and have her breakfast. She put on her red-pleated skirt with the yellow blouse and perched a bright blue beret on top of her curls.

"You look as gay as a farm cart," her father said.

"If you wander too far away over the fields you'll be spotted at once. That's why farm carts and wagons are painted so brightly. When the farmer is wanted in a hurry it's easy to pick him out among the green fields. It saves a long game of hide and seek."

Penny thought that was a very good idea, and she remembered how plainly she had seen the different machines dotted over the fields when she had walked with Maxwell across the hills above the farm. But it was a shame to cut short a game of hide and seek. On a farm there would be so many wonderful hiding places; not like the little garden at the back of her home where there was only the greenhouse and an apple tree. On a farm a game of hide and seek could last all day.

CHAPTER 2

THE LITTLE COW

PENNY had her breakfast and went to stand by the gate to watch for Maxwell's father. She didn't have long to wait. She closed her eyes and counted to ten, and when she opened them again a car was turning the corner of the street. As it came nearer, Penny saw that it wasn't just a car, but a car pulling a little trailer behind it. Penny wasn't sure that it was Maxwell's father, but when the car came closer Maxwell leaned out of the window and waved to her.

Maxwell's father was exactly like the farmer in all Penny's picture books: large and jolly, with a

round sunburned face and a loud booming voice. He greeted Penny's mother and father and told them to expect Penny back when they saw her. Then he told her to jump in the car. But something was moving around under the thick rope netting which covered the little trailer in the back, and Penny couldn't resist running over to see what it was. Something which looked like a toy cow lifted its head and stared back at Penny, and before she got over her surprise, a loud grunt made her look past the toy cow and straight into the black, beady eyes of a large white pig.

Maxwell called, "It's only an old sow. Come on."

"Why do you call it an old sow when it's a pig?" Penny said, climbing into the car beside him.

"Because that's what an old lady pig is called," Maxwell said.

"I love the little cow," Penny said. "I thought it was a toy."

"You mean the calf?" Maxwell said. "Don't call it a baby cow."

Maxwell's father said, "Maxwell's going to enjoy

showing off to you, I can see that. You mustn't let him get away with it all the time. He doesn't know everything."

But Penny didn't mind. She was in a new and exciting world and she was more than willing to listen to everything Maxwell could tell her and more than ready to look at everything he could show her.

CHAPTER 3

FAIRFIELD FARM

THE road to the farm wound up the hill, ran a little way along the top, and then wound its way down the other side. Just before they came to the bottom of the hill they arrived at a large white gate and Maxwell's father stopped the car for Maxwell to get out and open it.

FAIRFIELD FARM it said in large black letters on a board swinging by the gate.

"Don't forget to close the gate behind you," his father called after him. To Penny, he said, "That's one of the things Maxwell is *not* good at. He leaves gates open all the time. One of these days he'll do it once too often and we'll lose something."

18

On the other side of the white gate a wide, rough path bumped them across a cornfield to another gate, and this one led into the farmyard. It was just as if her picture books had come to life, Penny thought. Hens suddenly squawked and scattered in all directions. An old black sheepdog came bounding across the yard to meet them, and a horse nodded its head to them over a stable door.

Penny and Maxwell helped his father get the lady pig down from the trailer — and that wasn't easy. The old pig had decided that the trailer she knew was much safer than the farmyard she didn't know and she dug in her four short, strong legs and refused to move, squealing at the top of her voice. Penny thought she was silly. It would be so much fun in the farmyard with all the other animals to play with, but there was no way of telling that to the frightened pig. Her struggling protest started the little calf bucking and skipping and dodging, too, but at last the pig was down and scuttling through the doorway into the new sty to meet the father pig.

"And she'd better like him," Maxwell said, "or she'll be turned into bacon and sausages and ham."

Penny had never stopped to think that the bacon and sausages she ate for breakfast and the ham she sometimes had for dinner came from real pigs.

Maxwell laughed. "Where did you think they came from? You eat the hens and the ducks, too, *and* the cows and the sheep. Practically everything on the farm gets eaten sooner or later, and if it didn't everybody would starve."

"But not the little calf?" Penny said anxiously. "Don't let anyone eat the little calf."

Maxwell relented. "Well, perhaps not the little calf, as long as she grows up and gives lots of milk."

"Which she won't do if she stays in that trailer," Maxwell's father said. "Now if you want to be useful you can take her down to the field for me."

When she was out of the trailer and standing in the farmyard, the little calf didn't look any bigger than a large dog. She had a dark, curly, red-brown coat and a white face. She was friendly, too. If Penny had been alone with her she might have been the tiniest bit nervous, but with Maxwell between her and the baby cow she was quite brave.

"And please remember to fasten the gate," Maxwell's father called after them.

It was a nice field, and Penny was sure the little

calf would enjoy living there. It was a buttercup and daisy field, and Penny could have stayed there happily all morning, making daisy chains for the litle calf and gathering a bunch to take home.

"There isn't time," Maxwell said. "Now we have to collect the eggs."

He held the gate wide open and when Penny came running through he chased her down the lane and back to the farm just as if she were a small calf, too.

Behind them the gate swung back on its hinge, but not hard enough to latch itself to the post. Very slowly it swung open again.

CHAPTER 4

NO TIME FOR PLAY

THE little house where the hens lived had a tiny door at the front for the hens and a large door at the back for the farmer's wife. Penny followed Maxwell through the large door. It was dark and warm inside and, at first, Penny couldn't see anything at all. The hens, she thought, must be outside in the farmyard, but the next moment there was a great clucking and squawking, and hens were flying all around her in a most alarming way.

"It's all right," Maxwell said. "They were asleep. We surprised them."

"But they were on the *ceiling!*" Penny couldn't

understand why they had been so high above her head, unless *they* were playing hide and seek.

"They don't sleep in beds. They sleep on perches." Maxwell thought it was very funny that Penny didn't know that. Now Penny could see the perches, rows of them like steps reaching up the henhouse wall — not quite up to the ceiling, but almost.

"Don't they get tired standing up all night?" Penny asked.

"I shouldn't think so or they wouldn't do it," Maxwell said. He was used to seeing the hens like this all the time. To him it didn't seem odd at all.

But the nests were on the floor. They were all around the sides of the little house, deep comfortable hollows of soft straw. In some of the nests there were two eggs, and in some there was only one, and some of the eggs were deep brown like the one Penny had had for breakfast that morning, and some were white. Maxwell took the basket from a hook just inside the henhouse door and let Penny collect the eggs herself.

26

"And now it really is hide and seek to find the others," Maxwell said. "The hens won't all lay their eggs in the henhouse. Some of them like to lay them outside all over the place."

Penny thought that was great fun. It was just like Easter time when her mother hid her Easter egg, and she couldn't have it until she found it.

Penny found one egg in the stable, another by the haystack and another under the hedge. Maxwell found one in the barn and another in an old wheelbarrow — and that, he decided, was all.

The basket was full now and they took it back to the farmhouse, where Maxwell's mother was waiting to stack the eggs in boxes ready to be taken to market.

"Most of them but not all," Maxwell's mother said. "Here are a dozen I want you to take to Mrs. Polly at the Mill cottage, with this pound of butter and bottle of cream. I'll put them in the egg basket for you. Carry it carefully and go right there and back."

"Can Prince come, too?" Penny asked, her hand

on the silky head of the old sheepdog. He had scrambled to his feet the minute they came into the kitchen and had come bounding over to them.

"I'm afraid not," Maxwell's father said. "He has a job to do."

"A job?" Penny didn't understand. Dogs were to play with and to take on walks. She had never heard of their *working*.

"She has to take the cows back to the field when the milking's finished," Maxwell's father said.

"We'll take the cat then," Penny said as they crossed the farmyard. It was a large black cat with a sleek, shiny coat. She was sitting by the barn door washing herself, but the minute she heard their voices she came running over to them. She rubbed herself against Penny's bare legs, purring "Hello" in a very friendly way.

"You won't get her to leave the barn," Maxwell said. "She knows she has to catch mice."

"Everyone is *doing* something," Penny said. "When do we start to play?"

In her picture books the haystacks had looked

as if they had been made on purpose to slide down. Here in the farmyard there were several, all different shapes and sizes.

"The hay is for the cows and horses," Maxwell said. "If we mess it up it won't be any good for them to eat. How would you like someone trampling all over your breakfast?"

A family of ducks waddled across the yard in single file, Father Duck first, Mother Duck following, and behind them six fluffy yellow ducklings. From Penny's picture book they had looked up at her, asking to be played with, but now when she leaned forward to pick one of them up Father Duck turned around and spread his wings angrily.

"He won't let you play with them," Maxwell said. "They're on their way to their swimming lesson."

It was disappointing. The day on the farm wasn't turning out at all to be the kind of day Penny had imagined. Everyone was so busy. There didn't seem to be any time to play.

CHAPTER 5

THE WAY THROUGH THE WOODS

"I KNOW a short cut," Maxwell said. Maxwell's way would have got them to Mrs. Holly's cottage very quickly, except that he kept stopping to show Penny one exciting thing after another: frogs in a pool, a bird's nest in a hedge, a rabbit warren in a hillside. They stopped a long time watching the warren because as soon as Penny had looked at the carefully scooped-out holes which were the doorways to the warrens, she wanted to see a rabbit go in and come out of one.

"We'll have to hide then," Maxwell said. "If they see us or hear us they won't come anywhere near at all."

So they went to hide by a clump of bushes. They kept very quite and after a while out popped one rabbit from one hole, and then another from another hole. Penny had to cover her mouth with her hand to keep from laughing out loud. They looked so funny sitting there, still and sharp, ears pricked and listening. When they were satisfied there was no one near who would do them any harm they skipped happily away.

Penny would have liked to stay until they came back or until more came out, but Maxwell said it was almost dinnertime because the sun was shining right over their heads.

"I'm saving my allowance to buy a watch," he said, "so I'll know exactly what time it is all the time."

Penny only knew it was getting late because she was beginning to feel hungry.

Maxwell said, "We'll have to run."

But they couldn't run very fast without breaking the eggs in the basket or splashing the cream out of the bottle.

The last part of the way led through the woods. It was dark once they got inside and full of small, secret sounds: a rustling among the dried leaves, a fluttering in the branches of the trees, the distant snapping of a twig, little startled cries of birds. Penny kept very close to Maxwell and when he spoke to her she answered in a whisper.

"There's nothing to be scared of," Maxwell said. "It's only birds and rabbits. *We're* scaring them."

Penny hadn't thought of it like that and at once she began to feel less afraid. The woods didn't seem quite so dark now. Here and there the sun made bright patterns on the curled last-year leaves. Penny tried to walk only on the bright patches and soon it was a game, jumping from sunny patch to sunny patch.

"Wait for me," Maxwell called. He tried to run but in the basket the eggs chinked softly together, and a trickle of cream ran down the side of the bottle from under its paper cover.

"Try and catch me," Penny called back. Of all the games of hide and seek this was the best one.

"Wait for me," Maxwell called again, and this time his voice sounded fainter and farther away. Maxwell could never catch her, never, never, never. Penny stopped suddenly. She didn't really want Maxwell *never* to catch her. She just didn't want him to get ahead of her. She waited for him to come puffing and panting through the tangle of bushes and trees. She tucked herself behind an especially large tree so that she could jump out and surprise him when he came running up.

She waited, flattening herself against the rough bark of the tree and holding her breath so he wouldn't hear her and find her before she was ready to be found.

But there was no sound of Maxwell running, and no sound of Maxwell calling. Penny came out from behind the trunk of the tree and peered through the lacy branches. Now even the woods seemed to be listening, too. She stood the way the little rabbits had stood, quite still and hardly breathing. But unlike the little rabbits, she wanted someone to be near so that she could skip happily out to meet him.

In a moment she called, "Maxwell! Maxwell! Here I am."

She thought she heard Maxwell's voice calling back, ever so faintly and far away, but it might have been a wood pigeon calling from the far side of the woods.

She called again, louder. "Maxwell!"

This time not even the wood pigeon answered.

CHAPTER 6

THE MONSTER IN THE WOODS

MAXWELL was playing a game with her, Penny decided. He was hiding behind a tree as she had done. He was waiting for her to go and find him. She turned and ran back the way she thought she had come, but somehow it didn't look quite the same now. The trees seemed to be standing closer together and the bushes and brambles seemed to be twined more thickly across her path. She pushed her way through them, and they plucked and pulled at her red-pleated skirt and her bright yellow blouse.

She stood still again and called.

"Maxwell! I'm here. Come and find me!"

She waited another moment, listening to the soft, whispering voices of the wood and listening for Maxwell's voice, but he didn't call back to her. Then she knew that she would have to go and look for him.

She stood wondering which way to go. At that moment a twig snapped somewhere behind her. She spun around, and the sound came again, nearer. It was Maxwell creeping up to surprise her.

She called, "Here I am!"

There was a moment's startled silence and then a scrambling, splintering sound. This time something crashed through the woods in front of her, a long way in front of her so that she couldn't see exactly who or what it was, except that it was *not* Maxwell. It was something that looked brown one moment and white the next, something that was tall and long and fierce. She was quite sure it must be fierce. A fierce, wild monster! Penny's heart was thumping. Maxwell had said there were only birds and rabbits in the wood, but he didn't know everything. His father had said so. *This* was something he didn't know. Perhaps he had seen it, too, and had been frightened by it and had stopped chasing her to run back to the farm.

In a moment Penny would have been frightened, too, but the wild monster was running away from her, not toward her. The sound of scrambling and splintering and crashing got farther and farther away and in a very little while she couldn't hear it any more.

She started to breathe again. Now she knew what she was going to do. She would get out of the woods and go back to the farm where Maxwell would be waiting for her.

This time she didn't run off without looking where she was going. She took a careful look all around her, and at once she noticed something that she hadn't noticed before. One part of the woods was a lot brighter than the other part, as if the woods ended there and the rest of the world began again. That, she decided, was the way she would go.

CHAPTER 7

THE SAME — BUT NOT QUITE

PENNY picked her way very carefully, making no sound that might startle the wild monster again, and almost at once she came to the sunny patches. They were like bright stepping-stones which grew larger and larger and larger until at last she reached the edge of the woods and a lane which was very like the lane she had walked down with Maxwell and the little cow.

Almost — but not quite. The hedge that had surrounded the field had gone. In its place was a wire fence. Through the fence Penny could see across the field and there at the end of the field, at the foot of the hill, was the farmhouse.

40

She squeezed herself through the wire fence and began to run down the hilly field, but halfway across the field she stopped. The farmhouse didn't look quite the same. Instead of being long and low, it was narrow and tall. There were lots of stables and barns, but they all looked a different shape. And the carts and wagons in the farmyard were blue instead of red, and yellow instead of green.

Penny gazed around her. There was no other farmhouse in sight. This *must* be Maxwell's father's farm. It only looked different because she was looking at it from the hill. When she came closer it would look the same again.

She ran on, but the nearer she came the more different it looked. There was a little stream she hadn't noticed before, and a large wheel at the end of the tall, narrow house which turned in the water and made a splashing waterfall.

This must be the back of the farmhouse, Penny decided. The stream and the wheel had been there all the time, but she had been too busy looking at the pig and the little cow and the hens to notice it.

When she came to the end of the field she lifted the latch of the gate and walked into the farmyard.

An old sheepdog that was not Prince got slowly to his feet. A cat that was ginger instead of black arched her back, and at the same moment a man who was certainly not Maxwell's father came out of the tall, narrow house.

CHAPTER 8

THE SNOWMAN

AT first Penny thought the man was a walking snowman. His clothes were white, his cap was white, even his face and his hair and his eyebrows were white. But his eyes were blue and twinkling and his smile was friendly.

"What can I do for you?" he said.

Penny said, "I'm looking for my friend. We were playing hide and seek and he got lost."

"So he belongs to you, does he?" the man said. "I've tied him up in the barn. I thought someone would be looking for him sooner or later."

"You tied him up?" Penny was horrified.

44

"No telling where he might have gone if I hadn't, and doing damage all the time," the man said. "Look at my wife's flower bed. I don't know what she's going to say when she sees that."

Until that minute Penny hadn't noticed the little garden. It ran along the edge of the stream and was bright with pansies and marigolds and poppies. She could see that a lot of the flowers were broken and trampled down and there were deep, rough holes where the soil had been kicked away, but she couldn't believe what the man was saying.

"He — did that?" Penny said.

"That's right," the man said. "I'll be glad to have you take him home. I've given him a feed to keep him quiet."

"A feed!" Penny's voice was squeaky with astonishment.

"Ready for it, too," the man said. "You'd think he hadn't had a meal in days."

Penny couldn't understand it at all, unless Maxwell had got up so early to go to the market with his father that he had gone without his breakfast.

She followed the man across the farmyard and into the barn.

There was no sign of Maxwell. There was no one in the barn — except something that was brown and white and tall and long, but not a monster and not at all fierce.

The snowman saw the look of amazement on Penny's face and said, "Isn't this your friend?"

Penny shook her head. "My friend is a boy, Maxwell, but I didn't lose him. He lost me and then I lost the farm."

Now the snowman nodded his head understandingly. "Fairfield Farm." He stroked his chin thoughtfully. "You're pretty far away," he said. "I could take you back but right now I'm busy grinding corn. Suppose you come inside and tell me all about it. I know young Maxwell, and I've an idea it won't be long before he comes looking for you himself."

CHAPTER 9

LOST AND FOUND

WHEN Maxwell couldn't hear Penny any more he didn't know what to do at first. He knew she couldn't get very lost because it was only a little woods. If she came out on one side she would find herself back at the farm, and if she came out on the other side she would find herself on Mrs. Polly's doorstep. She must have gone back to the farm, he thought, because that was the way she knew. He would go back and find her there and then they would start all over again.

Maxwell stopped running this way and that way and went back to the path which was the shortcut.

He went down the hillside and past the rabbit warren, along the hedge where they had stopped to look at the bird's nest, around the pool where they had seen the frogs, and into the lane which ran past the farm.

When he got to the farm gate it was standing wide open, and in the yard his father was hitching the trailer to the back of the car again.

When he saw Maxwell he said, "Well, at least *you* aren't lost. Now you're here you'd better come with me to find her."

"I thought she'd be here. I came back for her," Maxwell said. "We lost each other in the woods."

For a second Maxwell's father looked puzzled, and then he guessed what must have happened.

"Don't tell me you've lost Penny, too," he said. "I'm bothered enough as it is about losing the new calf."

Now it was Maxwell's turn to look puzzled.

"*Someone* didn't close the gate properly," his father said, giving him a look. "The calf's wandered away, and now it seems Penny's wandered away, too. I'm too busy, you know, to be playing hide and seek. I thought you were old enough to be trusted."

Maxwell *was* old enough to be trusted, and he knew he should have known better than to leave the gate unfastened, but that was one of the things he was always forgetting. There were so many other things to think about.

Still holding the basket of eggs and butter and cream, he climbed into the car after his father. They drove off down the lane, which soon joined another lane which ran up a steep hill and around the woods. When they turned the corner at the top of the hill they could see the tall, narrow house and the little stream flashing in the sunlight. They could see something else, too — a little figure in a red-pleated skirt and a yellow blouse with a bright blue beret perched on top of her head.

Maxwell hung out of the window of the car, cupped his hands around his mouth and shouted, "Penny!"

The blustering wind caught at the word and

tossed it back into the woods where it got lost among the rustling leaves.

"It's no use shouting," Maxwell's father said. "The wind's blowing in the wrong direction. We'll go down and collect her first and then we'll try to find the little calf."

The lane was downhill all the way now. It didn't take long to get to the hump-backed bridge which spanned the river and led them right up to the yard which belonged to the tall, narrow house with its splashing water wheel.

Penny didn't know whether to be pleased because Maxwell had found her, or disappointed because she hadn't found him first.

"How did you know where I was?" she said.

"We could see you miles away," Maxwell said.

Penny looked down at her yellow blouse and bright red skirt and remembered what her father had said about being as gay as a farm cart and how she would be spotted at once if she wandered away.

"I'd like to stop a few minutes," Maxwell's father said to the snowman, "but I can't spare the

52

time. I bought a new calf in the market this morning. The children left the field gate open and she's strayed. You'd think I had nothing better to do than play games."

"You'd better spare the time to look at something in my barn," the snowman said. "Penny will show you."

Penny ran over to the barn and in a minute she came out leading the calf. "You found me," she said, "but I found the little cow."

CHAPTER 10

THE MILL COTTAGE

"WE'VE still got to find the cottage and give the eggs and butter and cream to Mrs. Polly," Penny said.

She couldn't understand why Maxwell was laughing, and why Maxwell's father was smiling, and why the snowman had such a twinkle in his eye.

"This is *Mr.* Polly," Maxwell's father said. "This is his mill."

"This is where we grind corn into the flour that makes the bread you eat," Mr. Polly said. "The cottage is right here, but on the other side of the mill. You've found it, but you've sort of come the back way."

"Someday," Maxwell's father said to Penny, "you must come and see Mr. Polly at work, but right now I have to get back to the farm. Run and get your errand done while Mr. Polly helps me lift the calf into the trailer." He called after Maxwell, "You'd better tell Mrs. Polly I'll make up the damage to the flower bed. Perhaps if I take it out of your allowance it will help you remember next time."

Maxwell thought sadly of the wrist watch which was almost his but which was now slipping another week farther away.

Mrs. Polly unpacked the basket and put the eggs, the butter and the cream away in her cool pantry.

"I don't like to see baskets going home empty," she said, coming back into the kitchen with a large, golden-brown, crusty loaf. "Just out of the oven. Tell your mother it's made with our flour," she said to Maxwell. "And here are a couple of buns to spoil your appetites for dinner."

The buns were warm from Mrs. Polly's oven, sticky with currants and smelling sweetly of spice. Mrs. Polly didn't know about the little trampled garden by the millstream and the broken flowers. Maxwell knew he had to tell her before he took the bun.

"Doors are made to open *and* shut," Mrs. Polly said, "but I seem to remember leaving a few open myself when I was your age. I still do, come to think of it. But I have what Mr. Polly calls a green thumb, so I shouldn't be at all surprised if I'm not able to straighten out most of those flowers again."

Penny looked at Mrs. Polly's thumbs, but they looked every bit as pink as her own.

"It doesn't mean her thumbs are *really* green, silly," Maxwell said. "It means that everything she plants grows."

Outside, Maxwell's father tooted the car horn.

"Come and see me again," Mrs. Polly called after them.

CHAPTER 11

TUPPENCE

W HEN they came to the buttercup and daisy field Maxwell's father lifted the little calf out of the trailer.

"I think we must christen it Maxwell," he said. "Maxwell the second."

"But Maxwell's a *he* and the little calf's a *she*," Penny said.

"All right," Maxwell's father said. "We'll call her Penny. How's that?"

Penny thought a moment and shook her head. She would have liked the little calf to be called by her name, but somehow it didn't seem to fit.

"She's almost twice as big as me," Penny said, "and she's got four legs instead of two."

"Tuppence, then," Maxwell's father said, and that name seemed exactly right.

Maxwell didn't think he would be allowed to help again but his father said, "Take her into the field. I don't think you'll forget to close the gate this time."

"I won't forget ever again," Maxwell said.

The little calf seemed glad to be safely back. She didn't stand sadly at the gate hoping to slip out after them again, but went bounding off through the shiny grass. This time she wasn't alone in the field. The other cows were back from the milking shed and were waiting to welcome her.

"She was lonely," Penny said. "She had no one to play with." Penny remembered how she had tried to run away once when she had first come from the city to live in the country. Then she had met the postman and the milkman and Maxwell, and she hadn't wanted to run away any more.

Dinner was in the big farmhouse kitchen. Prince

sat by Maxwell's father's chair and watched for the moment when he would get a tasty titbit from his master's plate. Penny had two helpings of everything in spite of the sticky currant bun, which had been the best bun she had ever tasted but which hadn't even begun to spoil her dinner.

In the afternoon they helped Maxwell's mother in the dairy. There was the cream to be separated from the milk, and then the cream to be churned into butter. The butter had to be weighed on the silver scales, slapped into the right shape, and then Penny was allowed to press a little picture onto each slab with the wooden marker.

Then it was teatime and after that it was time to go home.

Maxwell's father took Penny home. They went the long way around by the lane so that Penny could have a last look at Tuppence in her buttercup and daisy field.

"Good-by, good-by, good-by," Penny called, leaning out of the window of the car to wave to the little brown and white calf.

Tuppence was chasing a butterfly but when she heard Penny's voice she stopped and lifted her head.

"Good-by," Penny called again — and this time the little calf tossed her head. It was quite clear that she was trying to say: "Good-by. Come back soon."

They bumped and jolted down the lane and then they came out onto the road that wound up the hill and back to town.

"Did you have a happy time?" Penny's mother asked her.

Penny thought of all the things she had done since she had left home that morning: helping to get the old sow into her new sty, taking the little calf to the field, collecting the eggs from the henhouse and hunting for the ones that were hidden in the farmyard. Taking the basket of eggs and butter and cream to Mrs. Polly at the Mill cottage, and after that helping to make the butter, helping to slap it and wrap it so that it could be sold in the market next week.

"I've had a busy time," Penny said. "The animals aren't to play with. They have to work."

"It wasn't quite the way you expected it to be?" Penny's father asked.

"It was and it wasn't," Penny said. "I had an exciting time. We all got lost but we all got found again."

"Didn't you play any games at all?" Penny's mother said.

"It was one long game all the time," Penny said. "One long game of hide and seek."

64

Date Due

AP 6	FEB 8	MAY 14	
AP 20	NOV 30	SEP 29	
NO 30	APR 26	JAN 26	
MR 2	DEC 2	MAY 3	
MR 22	MAR 16	OCT. 13	
IR 23	NOV 15	OCT. 27	
AP 3		SEP. 19	
MY 17	JUL 81	OCT. 9	
SE 26	OCT 7	MAR. 23	
NO 28	OCT 7	FEB. 14	
DE 22	NOV		
APR 25	MAR 12		
OCT 8	SEP 19		
OCT 18	NOV 28		
OC 28 X	OCT 29		
NOV 19	NOV 26		
JUN 24 EB 10			
DEC 9 MAR 5			